T0116639

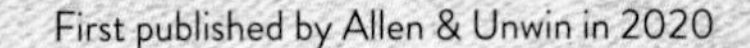

First published by Allen & Unwin in 2020

Allen & Unwin
83 Alexander Street
Crows Nest NSW 2065
Australia
Phone: (61 2) 8425 0100
Email: info@allenandunwin.com
Web: www.allenandunwin.com

A catalogue record for this book is available from the National Library of Australia

ISBN 978 1 76087 732 3

For teaching resources, explore www.allenandunwin.com/resources/for-teachers

Illustration technique: Watercolour on paper

Cover and text design by Arielle Gamble
Set in Brandon Grotesque 87pt
This book was printed in January 2020 by Everbest Printing Co., Ltd, China

1 3 5 7 9 10 8 6 4 2

The paper in this book is FSC® certified. FSC® promotes environmentally responsible, socially beneficial and economically viable management of the world's forests.

www.tashibooks.com

MY FIRST TASHI COLOURS

Anna & Barbara Fienberg
Kim Gamble, Arielle & Greer Gamble

In this world of
magic and mystery,
you can see . . .

RED
Tashi

BLUE

Genie

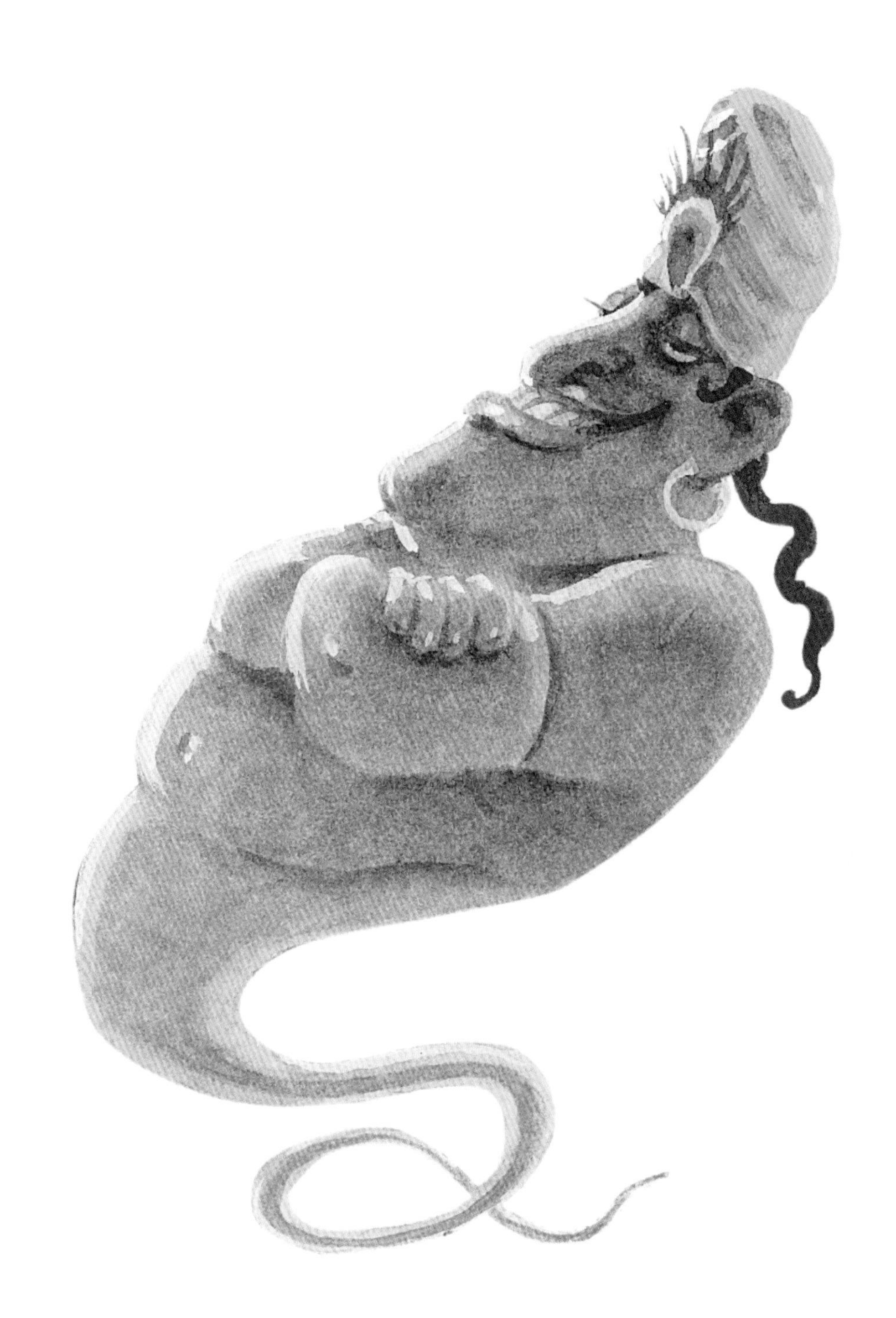

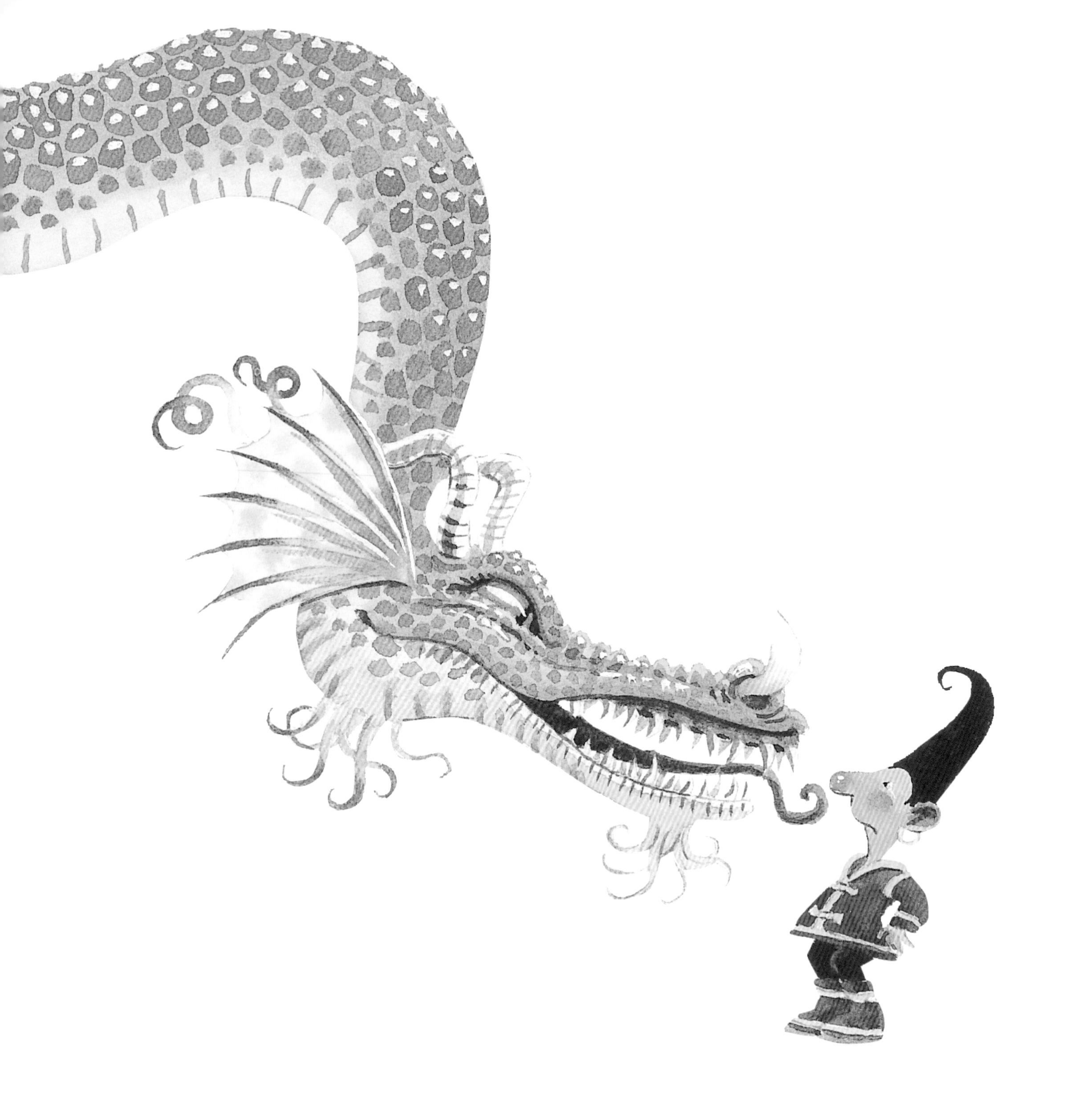

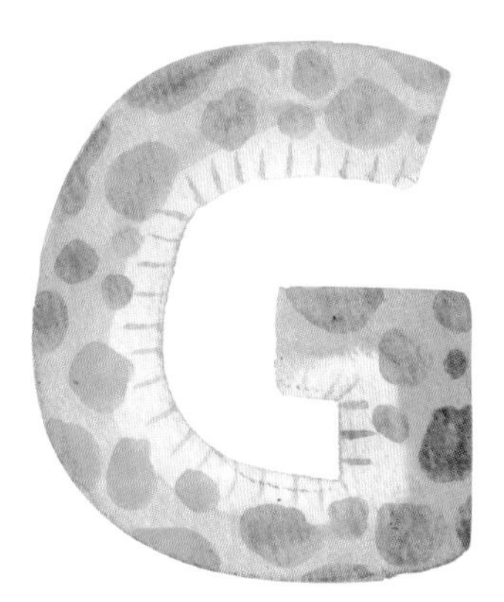

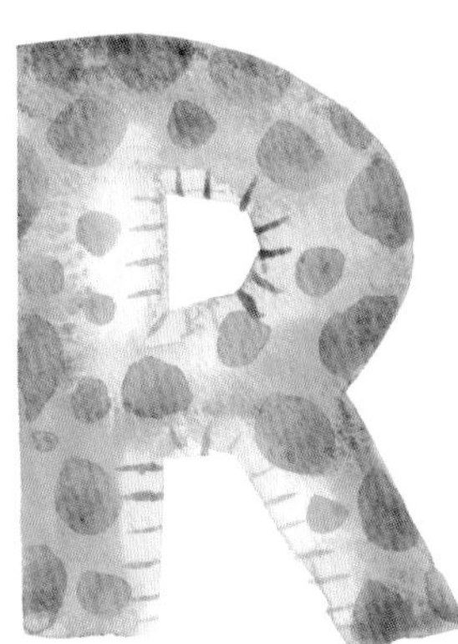

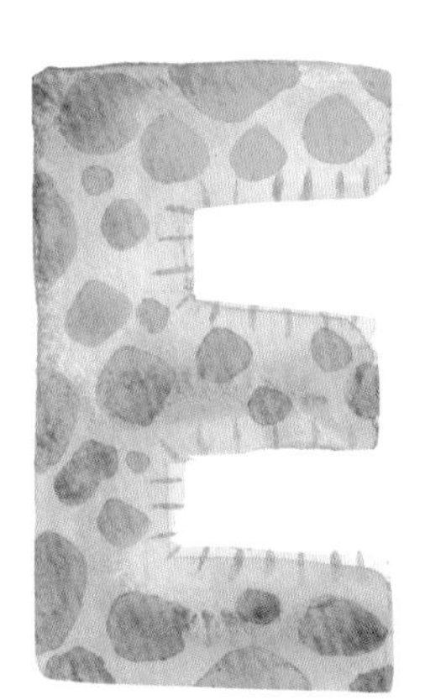

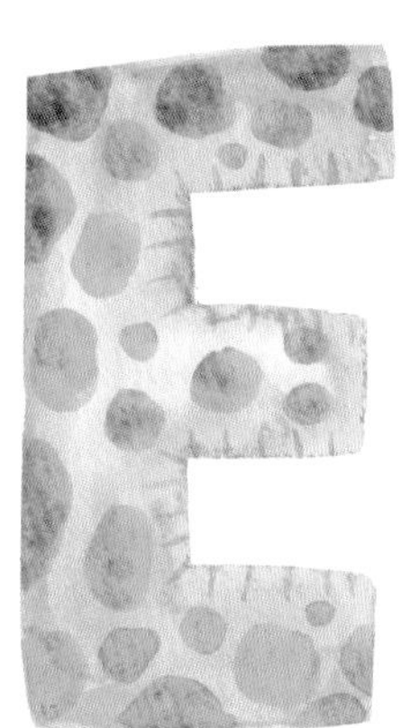

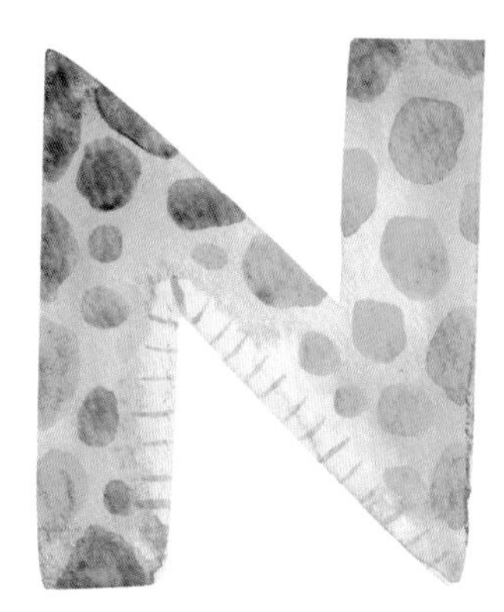

Dragon

YELLOW

Bus

SPECIAL

WHITE
Tiger

PINK
Pig

Horse

Baba Yaga

Sword

Treasure

and RAINBOW fireworks!

Tashi comes from two families, the Fienbergs and Gambles. My mother Barbara first saw him flying past on the back of a swan, so we brought him here to safety and gave him a best friend. And although Tashi told Jack the most marvellous tales, we didn't imagine Tashi would look very different from any other boy.

But when Kim Gamble got hold of him, Tashi turned from an ordinary boy who told magical tales into a magical boy. Kim shaped and dressed him, giving him a curious curl and a Santa Claus suit 'because Tashi carried magic gifts in his pockets'.

Tashi comes from a long line of storytellers. Since Barbara was very young, she told stories to entertain her friends (and get her out of trouble). And when she grew up to be a teacher librarian, she passed her passion for stories to me and hundreds of children as she read aloud to us in her library.

Kim too grew up loving stories, and drawing the heroes and baddies he found there. He also drew flowers when he couldn't contain his happiness. Kim and I met at *The School Magazine*. Our imaginations clicked and we went on to make scores of books. Like diving for a pearl, Kim reached in for the essence of a character, bringing it to the surface, extending feelings, transforming an idea into a world that was wilder and deeper than I'd ever realised.

I feel so lucky to have met this man, as do many thousands of children who've watched Kim draw a sunset, forests, moonlight over a river, all in the twenty minutes it took me to read the story.

And even though Kim is with us no longer, I am lucky that his exceptionally talented daughters have joined me now in Tashi's world. I've known and loved Arielle and Greer since they were little girls. From the time they were knee-high the girls' paintings hung amongst Kim's watercolours, blu-tacked up on his wall. As adults they've created their own paths across the artistic and literary landscape, and now they've brought their rich imaginations to join their father's, which has resulted in this truly family book.

We hope Tashi will become part of your family too.

Anna Fienberg